AMONG WOLVES

AMONG WOLVES

A STORY BY SCOTT O'CONNOR

THE SWANNIGAN & WRIGHT LITERARY MATTER

NEW YORK   CHICAGO   LOS ANGELES   OTHER PLACES

Published by **The Swannigan & Wright Literary Matter.**
Hernickers Swannigan: Publisher and Co-Founder
Oscar Wright: Publisher and Co-Founder [deceased]

www.thematter.net

This is a work of fiction. Any simularity between the
characters herein and any persons, living or dead,
is unintentional.

ISBN 0-9748479-1-7

Printed in the United States of America.

Book and cover designed by the author.

Second Edition, September, 2004

ONE

Here among wolves, here among pigs. Here among dogs and pirates. Here among dragons. Here among ghosts. Here among screaming children I sneak my first cigarette of the day.

I smoke it up in my head, so no one can see. I've taught myself to drag and inhale and exhale inside the big, fuzzy head, without raising a paw, without ever having to touch the cigarette.

Smoking in costume, on the midway, in sight of the visitors, is frowned upon. Is obviously not the best idea if you want to keep your job. Your job as Diggity Dawg. So I smile at the kids and wave at the kids and bend to the sides, left and right, left and right, in a rough approximation of diggity dancing, while inside my giant head I exhale smoke in tiny streams through the holes in my sad, dopey eyes. No one's the wiser.

While I'm smoking and dancing, left and right, left and right, I keep an eye out for him. Always looking.

That could be him, standing over by the

pay phones. The tall older gentleman, with the lean, military build. With the brush cut, with the neatly-trimmed mustache, with the aviator sunglasses. With the pipe in his mouth.

I move towards him to get a better look and the cigarette slips. It falls into the seam where my dog head meets my dog body.

This is not good. My dog head's filling with smoke. I shake both my heads, one inside the other. I box my floppy ears as if my entire head is on fire.

Everything's going gray. I'm choking on the smoke. A cough sneaks up from my chest and out of my mouth. One of the kids in the crowd stops screaming and turns and looks up at me. Smoke is coming out my ears. I can see it curling back around into my rapidly diminishing line of sight. The kid's about to scream again, a new scream, a scream about the smoke coming out of Diggity Dawg's ears. I hold a fuzzy finger up to my mouth and blow. *Shhhhhh*. A stream of smoke exits the head's mouth hole with the shush. The kid's eyes go wide. He takes a deep breath, holds it, and screams bloody murder.

Parents turn. Kids turn. Wolves and pigs and dragons turn. I'm wobbling around, light-headed, nearly blind. The kids run out of the way, afraid I'll topple. It must look like I'm about to explode, like I've got a bomb with a sizzling fuse in my head.

A hand on my shoulder. One of the pirates. He grabs hold of my right paw and drags me off the midway, away from the kids. I can't see a thing. I'm staggering drunkenly, twisting and trailing smoke like a failing plane. I try to find the man by the pay phones. The man with the pipe. I shake my heads again, moving smoke around, trying to clear my vision. The pirate is pulling and it's hard to keep my feet.

As we get to the door of the office, I find him again. Over by the pay phones, watching the commotion, tapping the stem of his pipe against his bottom teeth.

It's not him. I thought it might be, but it's not.

The pirate pulls me into the office and

slams the door behind us.

I don't really know what he'd look like now. I don't know how much he might have changed. I still picture him looking like he did eight years ago.

Here he is. Here we are. Here's our house—a white split-level on a quiet street with other white split-levels, with fences between them, with vegetable gardens and swing sets in the back yards. It's a beautiful Saturday morning, sunny and clear and warm. There's one week until summer vacation. Two weeks until my birthday. Number ten. Cartoons on the TV in the living room. A commercial break.

He's in the garage. The garage door is open, laying flat across the ceiling in its metal brackets. He's lying on the cement floor, grunting and groaning, pipe clenched in his teeth. His forehead and mustache are wet with sweat. His long legs kick out onto the newly blacktopped driveway. I'm standing over him, watching.

He's fixing the lawn mower. The lawn mower is flipped on its side. His face and hands are pressed into the grass-clogged blades. His jeans and white t-shirt are smeared with grease. He's struggling with a ratchet and a bolt.

This is the last moment, the very last second I can remember when everything was as it should have been.

And then.

Look:

Wait. Not yet. There's something else you need to know. To understand. Some family history.

The year before, the four of us had driven down to Florida. My dad, my mom, my sister Margot and me. Piled into our Pontiac station wagon. The annual family vacation. Lots of luggage. I was small and chubby. I had a head of hair like Harpo Marx. It looked like a clown wig, or a burning bush. Margot was 13. She had a dark brown birthmark that covered her right cheek and some of her neck. It looked like she had spilled a cup of coffee on herself.

The drive took three 10-hour days. The

"scenic route." Winding country roads and rutted small town streets. My dad hated highways. My dad hated the Eisenhower Interstate System. His job was: County Roads Supervisor. His job was about: local thoroughfares.

We never broke the speed limit. The speed limit was never more than 45. My dad kept a golf pencil and a pocket-sized spiral notebook on the dashboard. He never played golf, but he said that erasers made you lazy. He recorded the names and conditions of each road we turned down and the miles traveled on each in his neat, labored capital letters.

We drove down through Ohio and into Kentucky and Tennessee. My dad wanted to visit Graceland. We didn't go inside, because the admission fee was too expensive. We had our picture taken standing at the front gate.

We stayed in roadside motels that were listed in the AAA *Traveler's Guide*. No less than one star but no more than three. One room, two beds. Margot and my mom shared a bed. My dad and I shared a bed. My dad and I wore white undershirts with matching yellow stains under the arms. My shirt was too big. It hung to my knobbly knees.

We ate dinners at the little coffee shops attached to the motels, in booths between the booths of traveling salesmen and the line of long-distance truckers sitting at the counter. Two of the motels we stayed at had in-ground pools by the parking lots. One of the pools had water in it. After dinner at the coffee shop, I splashed around in the shallow end while Margot had my mom rate her dives into the deep end. The dives never rated higher than: 8.5. Margot wore her new swimsuit. The salesmen and truckers stood out by the door of the coffee shop and smoked cigarettes and watched Margot dive. My dad spread out in a plastic chaise lounge a safe distance from the water with his *Traveler's Guide*. He studied the next leg of the trip. He jotted things down in his notebook.

At night we lay on top of the beds in our motel room and watched strange local channels with unfamiliar newscasters. Margot and I saw cable TV for the first time. We watched PG movies on HBO. My dad went down the hall to the vending machines and returned with cans of soda and handfuls of candy bars. My mom disapproved but the 1,000 Grand won her over.

When my dad's watch said 9:30, he switched off the lights. At home I went to bed at 9:30, and he said that since we only had one room we all had to go to bed at 9:30. At the motel by Graceland, we told him that it was really 8:30. That it was Central Time. But my dad didn't believe in time zones. He thought they were a load of bunk.

We got up every morning at dawn. My dad packed the car while my mom collected our things and straightened the room. She'd brought along a spray can of disinfectant and a package of sponges. She cleaned the shower and the toilet. She made the beds. She left a fifty-cent tip on the dresser for the maid.

Margot was often carsick in the morning. She had to ride with her eyes closed and her head down between her knees in a large mustard-yellow bucket. She never threw up, though we thought she might. My mom reached back from the front seat and rubbed Margot's head while Margot coughed and spit into the bucket.

My dad and mom and I ate breakfasts in roadside diners while Margot moaned out in the car. We got sandwiches and sodas to go for lunch. Margot always felt better by noon. We'd pull off into a gravel turnaround or grocery store parking lot and Dad would lower the back gate of the station wagon and we'd sit in a row on the gate and eat our egg salads on wheat and drink our grape Fantas. Margot always ordered her sandwich without mustard. She said the color made her sick.

Margot and I brought a Sears cassette recorder along on the trip. A Christmas gift from Mom and Dad. It had a microphone on a long black cord that plugged into the back. We interviewed each other as we drove along, pretending that we were famous. We made up game shows. My dad was the host, with his rumbling baritone. We sang travel songs. *On the Road Again*, *Move it On Over*. We played the tape back and laughed at the sound of our disembodied voices.

On the third day, we arrived at the Park.

Margot started complaining again. She was embarrassed that we were going to this theme park instead of the other one, the famous one. My dad said that the famous park was overpriced. My dad said that the famous park was a rip-off. Margot kept complaining. She said that the kids at school would make fun of her when they saw the pictures. She said that nobody had ever heard of this park. My dad said then that makes it Our Park.

I loved Our Park. I loved the strangeness of it. I loved how I didn't recognize the names of the rides or any of the characters wandering the midway. Everything was there to be discovered. I wanted to run through the park, touching each sign and ticket booth and concession stand to make it mine.

We spent three days in the park and three nights at the motel across the street from the front gate. Then it was time to leave. On the way home, we stayed at the same motels and ate at the same restaurants as the way down. My dad recorded it all in his notebook.

The pirate pushes me inside Jensen's office. He shuts the door behind us and starts tugging at my head. I grab onto the doorknob and brace myself and he gets a hold of my big floppy ears and pulls.

My head finally pops off. A big cloud of smoke, loose in the office. I gag and choke and wipe at my eyes. The cigarette falls to the floor, still lit. The pirate crushes it out with his peg leg. Jensen yells at him to open a goddamn window. The pirate opens a goddamn window. Jensen gets up and turns on an air-conditioning unit. The air-conditioner rattles to life. Jensen waves his meaty hands around to clear the smoke. He sits back behind his desk. Goddamnit, he says.

The office is a cramped and cluttered trailer. Single-wide. It sits back behind the first-aid station, out of sight of the midway and the visitors. One whole end of the trailer is crammed with a forest of wooden signs that need to be repaired or repainted. You must be this high to enjoy this ride. Open boxes of Christmas decorations sit on the floor around Jensen's desk. Stacks of employee handbooks and overstuffed file folders teeter on top of the little stove in the kitchenette. There's a poster tacked to the wall explaining Florida's minimum wage law and Your Rights as an Employee.

None of the furniture is office furniture. Per se. Jensen's chair and the chair on my side of his desk are really high-backed dining room chairs, but not from the same set. The desk looks like a little kid's desk. It looks like the desk I used to have when I was a kid. Jensen's knees stick up over the top. His gray slacks. A fluorescent overhead light buzzes along with the air conditioner. Ten dead flies in the light's plastic casing.

Jensen tells me to put my pack of cigarettes on the desk. I unzip my costume and pull the pack from the waistband of my underpants and put it on the desk.

Jensen gives me a lecture about how we aren't supposed to smoke in costume. You know this, Blaylock, you know this. I know, I know, I say, wringing my hands, googling my eyes, but I'm an addict and I have a problem. Jensen doesn't laugh. The pirate laughs and Jensen shoots him a look and the pirate stops laughing. I don't recognize the pirate. He must be the new shift supervisor. He's got his eye patch up on his forehead. He's got mean, squinty eyes. One of his front teeth is blackened to make it look like it's missing. He scratches around his knee, where it fits into the wooden peg.

Jensen tells me that I very nearly caused a Safety Incident. He tells me that I'm a fuck-up but that I have a way with the kids, though God knows he wouldn't let his kids anywhere near me. He tells me that because of my way with the kids he's not going to tell the higher-ups and that I'm lucky because if he told the higher-ups I'd be out on my ass. He tugs at the knot of his tie and says goddamn that smoke, Ilford. Ilford must be the pirate. Ilford gives a little cough to show Jensen that he sympathizes.

Jensen tells me that this is my last warning. He tells me that he believes in rehabilitation over punishment but that he's no fool in that regard. That there will be some punishment and the punishment is that I'm going to have to stay late tonight and help the fucking Cubans put up the Christmas in July decorations. Ilford laughs when Jensen says fucking Cubans.

I ask is that all and Jensen says no that's not all and to watch my tone when I speak to him. Then he doesn't say anything and I don't say anything and Ilford doesn't say anything and finally Jensen looks at his watch and tells me to go to lunch. I say yes, sir, and Jensen says I told you watch your fucking tone. Sorry, sir. Ilford hands me my head and opens the door. I step outside, into the sun. Right before Ilford closes the door behind me, Jensen says something under his breath, but loud enough for me to hear. What he says is: *crazy faggot*.

I turn back around and knock on the door. Ilford opens it and I ask can I have my cigarettes back. Jensen yells no you can't have your fucking cigarettes back and Ilford close that goddamn door. Ilford shrugs and closes the door in my face.

* * *

So this is the part. The important part. The part that led to that morning in the garage.

The night before, there had been a professional wrestling event at the War Memorial downtown. I was a big fan. I watched the professional wrestling show on TV every Saturday morning, after cartoons. I rooted for the bad guys. They were more interesting than the good guys. I rooted for "Rowdy" Roddy Piper. I rooted for the Iron Sheik. I wondered if they had wives and kids and if the wives and kids knew they were bad guys, and if the wives and kids were disappointed because they always lost.

For a couple of weeks before that night, the announcer "Mean" Gene Oakerlund would break into the action of the show with a spot about the upcoming local event. I'd never been to see the wresting show live. I wanted to go, desperately. I left hints for my dad. I cut out the nightly ad from the newspaper and put it in his brown bag lunch in the morning, or in his copy of *U.S. News and World Report*, replacing the subscription card. I brought the upcoming local event up, out of the blue, at dinner. I tried to engage Dad in debates about my favorite wrestlers, and then mentioned the fact that they would soon be appearing live and in person at our own War Memorial.

Dad could have cared less about wrestling. Dad was a baseball man, and a hockey man. He'd played both when he was my age. By the time he was in high school he was the best player on the diamond and the ice in his hometown. We had a framed black and white picture of him on the fireplace mantle in the living room—a strapping, smiling teenager, proudly showing his missing tooth, holding a gigantic trophy over his head. I don't know if it was a baseball trophy or a hockey trophy. The picture cut off at the bottom before you could see if he was wearing skates or cleats.

I played Little League during the summer. My dad took me to the weekday evening practices and Sunday afternoon games. I couldn't field a line drive or get a base hit to save my life. The coach planted me in deep right field, out by the concession stand. If there was even the slightest possibility that someone on the other team would hit the ball that far, he planted me on the bench. I tried to keep out of the way of the real players.

The only sport I liked was wrestling. But I knew. I knew that my dad thought there was something not right about watching it. Oiled-up men wearing only swim trunks, rolling around, hands all over each other. Pulling. Biting. So I didn't ask him to take me to the War Memorial. In so many words. I hoped that he'd get the hints.

Whenever my parents wanted to surprise Margot and me, they would leave the surprise on the kitchen table in the morning, so we would find it when we came downstairs for breakfast. Birthdays went like this. Christmas went like this. The Sears cassette recorder. The vacation to Florida went like this—my dad left copies of the route and itinerary under our cereal bowls one morning a few months before the trip.

But on the morning of the live local event, there were no tickets sticking out from under my cereal bowl at breakfast. I lifted the bowl and looked to see if maybe they'd been pushed all the way under. I lifted Margot's bowl. She hissed at me and slapped my hand away.

When I got home from school, there weren't any tickets waiting in my room, on my pillow or my bookshelves. When my dad got home from work, he didn't take me aside and whisper in my ear. Dinner wasn't scheduled early so we could get downtown by seven o'clock, by bell-time. The surprise never came.

After dinner, I went up to my room. I could hear my dad reading the paper down in the living room—clearing his throat, turning the pages, shaking them out so they'd stand up straight. Just a regular night. Nothing special. I sat on my bed and tried not to cry.

Finally, I smelled his pipe outside my door. The sweetness of the tobacco. He came into my room and sat beside me on the edge of my bed. He had to move some of my stuffed animals to make space. He explained that the tickets had been too expensive, that we just couldn't afford them. I cried. I tried not to, but I did.

He stood up and gave me his handkerchief. I wiped my eyes and my nose and held the handkerchief up to give it back, but he wasn't looking at me. He was looking around my room at the shelves of books and piles of stuffed animals and cut-out magazine photos of my favorite wrestlers taped to the walls. There wasn't a single trophy. There wasn't a single sports pennant. The only thing I'd ever won was a small wooden plaque from a science fair sponsored by the local chapter of the Rotarians. I'd researched a number of topics—heart attacks, strokes, the effects of household poisons on human beings—before my teacher suggested Chewing and Swallowing in Mammals. I'd built a human head out of paper mache. When you put jellybeans in the mouth and moved the jaw, it looked like the head was chewing. But I could never get the head to swallow and so the jellybeans always fell out of the mouth and clattered on the floor. The gold-plated sign on the plaque read: *Third Place*.

I couldn't stop crying. I was disappointed and embarrassed. My dad was disappointed and embarrassed. He thought that I was the third girl in the family. I knew this.

He went back downstairs. I sat down at my desk and turned on my computer. It was a second-hand model we'd bought at a neighbor's garage sale. It was hooked up to a small black and white TV.

I had a program where you could type in a word or phrase and the computer would say it back, out loud, in a metallic robot voice, through the little speaker on the TV. And what I did was I typed *I hate you* into the computer and hit *Return* and the computer said *I hate you* in its hollow monotone.

I typed it again and hit *Return* again. *I hate you*. I turned up the volume knob on the TV and typed it again. *I hate you*. I turned up the volume some more. *I hate you*. Again and again, louder and louder.

Who I was typing it to: both of us.

I heard him coming up the stairs. The floor creaking. The pipe smell. I turned the TV up as loud as it could go. *I hate you*. He came around the corner. He closed my door and went back downstairs without saying a word.

I cried even harder. Big, wracking sobs. I did not think he deserved that. But, at that very moment, downtown: "Rowdy" Roddy Piper, The Iron Sheik. Live and in person.

Big, wracking sobs.

I cried myself to sleep.

I woke up on Saturday morning and knew that it had passed, that it was over. During the night, the workers had taken down the lights, disassembled the ring, packed the eighteen-wheelers. The wrestlers had boarded buses and planes for the next city. The hours spent crying in my bedroom seemed selfish and unnecessary. I was sorry. I wanted him to know.

I sat on the living room floor in front of the cartoons on TV and screwed up my courage. I didn't have much to screw up. During a commercial, I went downstairs to the screen door and watched him struggling with the lawn mower in the garage.

If I had known anything about baseball, I would have talked about that. If I had known anything about County Roads, I would have talked about those. But all I could think about was the trip to Florida, to Our Park. It was something we both knew. It was something we shared.

We had done this before. Whenever I was sad or scared or upset he would dig out his little spiral notebook and recount details—street names, miles traveled, amounts paid for sandwiches and grape Fantas. I would ask an easy question and he would answer and we would recount the entire trip, day by day. The exactitude, the certainty of the details, always made me feel safe.

I thought that if we could talk about the trip, maybe he'd forget what I had done. Maybe he'd ask me to help him fix the lawnmower. Maybe he'd ask me to get specific tools and hand them to him. The ratchet set, the Philips head screwdriver.

I opened the screen door. I asked a question. An easy one, a slow pitch.

"Dad, on the trip to Our Park in Florida, do you remember where we were all supposed to meet if anybody got lost?"

"Ummm." He talked around the stem of

the pipe clenched in his teeth. He didn't look up from the lawnmower blades. "The roller coaster, right?"

He was distracted. He was still angry.

"No," I said. "That wasn't it."

"Must have been the clock then." He grunted, struggling to loosen a bolt. "That giant clock."

"There's no giant clock at Our Park," I said.

"Well then it must have been the roller coaster, honey." He tried to push his face further into the mower to better see the bolt, but his pipe kept getting in the way. He took it out of his mouth and held it up for me. "Can you put this over on the shelf?"

I took the pipe. The plastic mouthpiece on the end of the stem was wet and scored with his toothprints. I put it in my mouth and tried to fit my teeth into his marks. They wouldn't fit. Either the prints were too big or my teeth were too small. I took the pipe out of my mouth and put it on the shelf next to his ratchet set.

"Don't you remember?" he said. "You

wanted to go on the roller coaster but you were too little." He hammered at the handle of the ratchet with his fist, but the bolt wouldn't give.

"No," I said. "That didn't happen."

"Sure it did," he said.

"No," I said. "It didn't."

I hated roller coasters. The open space terrified me. He knew this.

"I don't kno-ow," he said, sing-songing the word. "I seem to remember someone getting pretty upset because he was too small to go on the ride."

What my dad knew: everything. He knew the length and breadth of every paved road in the county. He knew the length and breadth of every unpaved road in the county. He knew the weekly top-ten American League batting leaders and their on-base percentages. And he knew the trip to Our Park, minute by minute, mile by mile.

But this was not true, this story about the roller coaster. This had never happened. This was a fabrication.

He tugged on the ratchet. He grunted as he

tugged.

I watched the back of his head while he worked. From up there, standing above him, it looked like a stranger's head. His thick brown hair had little trails of gray above the ears. I'd never seen them before. Squirming around on the floor, wrestling with the bolt, his body moved in weak, unfamiliar ways. His arms shook with the strain. He kicked his legs. My dad had never moved that way.

He gave the ratchet a good knock with his fist and the bolt finally jerked to the left. "Christ," he breathed. He spun the ratchet around in an easy circle until the bolt dropped out. He was breathing hard, wheezing. He cracked a couple of coughs into his fist.

"Why the third degree, Joe Friday?" he asked. "Working on your memoirs?" Even his voice sounded different—a tick higher in pitch.

"I'm writing a paper for school," I lied. "And I need to get the facts right."

You know how if you say your name out loud, over and over and over again, after a while it stops making sense? It's not your word anymore. It's not a word at all anymore. It's just a meaningless sound. I was staring at him so hard in the garage, that's how he began to feel to me. He stopped making sense. Everything about him seemed strange.

"Could you hand me my pipe, Honey?" he said.

I took the pipe from the shelf and handed it to him. He struck a match and touched it to the tobacco. He took a puff. He grabbed my knee and gave it a squeeze and lay back down to look for the next bolt. He fitted the ratchet to it and tugged to the left.

"You can trust my memory, Honey," he said. "Would your Old Man steer you wrong?"

He gave the ratchet a good pull and the bolt turned to the left and the whole world followed. It came off its rails, just a bit, just a fraction, but enough so that I could see it was all wrong, that all the fake things, all the masks and scenery, had slipped. I grabbed. I grabbed but it was out of reach.

My dad would never steer me wrong. I knew that. He never had and never would.

But my dad had never called himself "your Old Man" in his life.

I felt someone watching me. Eyes on the back of my neck. I turned around and saw them through the screen door, standing side-by-side at the top of the stairs: someone who looked like my mom, with her curly red hair, with her mismatched eyes, one green and one blue; someone who looked like Margot, with her coffee stain. They stared back at me, expressionless. And then the girl who looked like Margot slowly lifted a finger and put it to her lips and blew. *Shhhhh.*

I felt something cold and wet and alive start crawling up my spine.

What I knew then: this wasn't my dad, this wasn't my mom, this wasn't Margot.

What I knew then: imposters.

My family had been replaced by imposters.

It's hot today, even hotter than usual, and for a second I wish I had a job where I could wear short-sleeved shirts or shorts or even light slacks—anything but a big furry dog costume. I'm only wearing underpants underneath, but it's still over a hundred degrees inside this thing.

I thought the employee cafeteria would be empty because it's so early, but most of the tables are full of cats and dogs and dragons finishing up breakfast or starting lunch. I always bring my lunch. My lunch is always: egg salad on wheat. Lots of mustard.

I add my Diggity Dawg head to the row of disembodied heads at the end of a table and take a seat next to a decapitated moose. I'm not a big talker, so I don't really know anybody at the table, but they don't seem to mind that I'm sitting here, or that I smell like charred synthetic fur. Compared to what some people smell like in these costumes, charred fur isn't so bad.

A shadow falls across our lunches. Everyone at the table stops talking and stiffens in their seats. I look up. Ilford is standing on the other side of the table, looking down at me. There's a red and green plastic parrot perched on his shoulder. He's got his patch back down over his eye.

"Yar," he says.

"Hey," I say.

"Jensen was real fuckin' pissed," he says. He's got some kind of Irish accent or something, so it sounds like *fookin' pissed*. "He says you're a real fuck-up." *Fook up*.

I start to say something, but a panda at the end of the table gives me a big-eyed warning look. Like, Just keep quiet. Ilford sees me look at the panda and so he looks at the panda. "What're you lookin' at?" he says. The panda looks back down into his creamed corn.

"That sounds about right," I say to Ilford.

"What sounds about right?"

"That I'm a fuck-up."

Ilford throws his head back and laughs, showing his blackened tooth. "Yar," he says. "I guess you're right!" The parrot falls off his shoulder and he stoops to pick it up. *Fookin' bird*. He gets the parrot and stands and puts my cigarette pack on the table.

"Hope you don't mind, Blaylock," he says, "but I helped myself to a couple." I can tell by the way he says it that he doesn't really care if I mind or not.

"How many?" I ask.

Everybody at the table stiffens again. Someone down at the end lets out a little disbelieving grunt.

"How many?" he says. Ilford's uncovered eye narrows. Then he throws his head back and his face splits in another laugh. "Jesus, Blaylock, you're a real tosser, you know that?" *Jaysis, Blaylock*.

"Yeah," I say. "That sounds about right. How many?"

"How many!" Guffaw, guffaw, guffaw. "Three, Blaylock! I pinched three of your cigarettes! Ah, you fuckin' kill me!" He adjusts the parrot on his shoulder and turns from the table to go. "Have fun with the fuckin' Cubans tonight, you tosser!"

The moose next to me looks like he's Cuban or something and when he hears this he starts to get up. He's showing his teeth like he's going to eat Ilford, like he's going to sink his teeth into Ilford's throat. But the panda at the end says, Let it go, man, and the moose closes his mouth and sits back in his chair.

"Asshole," the moose mutters.

I ask the moose to unzip the back of my suit. I tuck the cigarette pack into the waistband of my underpants and the moose zips my suit back up and we all go back to eating our lunches in silence.

I remember a commotion downstairs that night, while "Rowdy" Roddy Piper and the Iron Sheik teamed up at the War Memorial, while I cried up in my room. Some yelling, some banging around. I'd assumed it was Margot vs. my parents, arguing over her curfew or her choice of friends or the amount of time she spent on the phone. But that was the night of the imposters. The night they removed my family and took their places. And I cried through the whole thing. My dad and mom and sister were dragged off, kicking and screaming for help and I cried through the whole thing.

I had no idea why imposters had replaced my family. Why any group or organization with such impressive and thorough powers of disguise would take an active interest in disrupting the life of a nine-year old boy in the suburban Midwest. The cost alone, in mimicry training and prosthetics, would have been staggering. Not to mention the commitment necessary, the dedication of the agents, the willingness to assume someone else's existence for however long the mission required.

But after that morning in the garage it became clear that they were not who they pretended to be. These people. Their behavior was completely off.

Almost every afternoon that summer when "Dad" got home from work, he'd suggest we go out to the back yard and work on some fielding. Fly balls. Line drives. My real dad never had the patience for that. He got frustrated because I never got any better. But this man stood out by the swing set with my dad's aviator sunglasses on and my dad's pipe in his mouth and slapped out hit after hit. I'd chase the ball's shadow across the yard and try not to get whacked in the head when it fell from the sky.

This man never got frustrated. He kept shouting things like, "Good try, son," and "Way to hustle," after I'd fallen on my face or run into the fence. When "Mom" would call us in for dinner, he'd wait by the back door as I limped up the yard in my grass-stained jeans. He'd put his arm around my shoulders and clomp me on the head with his glove.

He took me to the Little League games on Sunday afternoons. While I was up at the plate, whiffing away, he'd be standing in the bleachers, hands cupped around his mouth, yelling, "Hang in there, Blaylock!" and "Just make contact!" The other parents stared at him. They thought he was wasting his breath. After I'd struck out, he'd clap and yell, "Next time, slugger! Next time!"

After one at bat, Jimmy Fargus, our All-

Star first baseman, spoke to me for the first time all season. He asked me who that guy was. I told him, honestly, that I didn't know.

The woman who played "Mom" was just as unconvincing in her role. She was harder and colder than my real mother. She had less patience and a quicker temper. She glared at "Dad" suspiciously when he came home late from work and snapped at him over the littlest things. Almost every night I could hear her crying behind the closed door of their bedroom while "Dad's" muffled voice tried to comfort her.

And she was trying to poison me.

I was sure of this. I realized it one morning at breakfast when my raisin bran tasted strangely medicinal. A half hour later, I was throwing up in the bathroom. I never threw up, even when I was really sick. The only explanation that made any sense was poison.

From then on, whenever "Mom" set a bowl of cereal or plate of pancakes on the table in front of me and turned back to the stove, I would pretend to take a bite.

"Mom?" I'd ask, almost choking on the word. "Do these taste funny to you?"

I could see it in her eyes as she crossed back to the table. The hatred and frustration. I'd escaped again. But it was no more than a flicker before her "Mom" mask was back in place and she was taking my spoon or fork and taking a bite and smiling sweetly and saying, "No, dear. It tastes fine to me."

She never swallowed. I never saw her swallow. And I knew about swallowing, third place or no. She'd turn back to the stove and I'd listen for the sounds of the mandible shift, the masseter contraction, the tensing of the superior pterygoid, the working of the throat. Nothing. At night I would check the soil in the potted plants on the kitchen windowsill for half-chewed pancakes or raisin bran, but she must have cleared them out when I wasn't looking.

At dinner, I never ate unless the others were eating from the same serving bowl or dish and chewing and swallowing. Very important, watching them swallow. The stare-downs we had at the kitchen table, seeing who would swallow first. I lost nine pounds that summer. "Dad" punched a new hole in my leather Star Wars belt.

"Margot" was the least successful at playing her part, but it's been my experience from working at the Park that child actors aren't ever very good.

She became even more sullen and withdrawn than the real Margot. She spent most of her time in her room, on the phone with "friends." I always assumed she was being taken to task for her poor performance by whoever was in charge of the operation. When I'd ask who she was talking to, she got angry. She didn't even try to hide her contempt for me. It was laughable.

The only times she was even the least bit believable was when she would "argue" with my "parents", screaming and yelling from the top of the stairs and then running back to her room, slamming everything she passed—drawers, windows, her bedroom door. You could even hear her crying in there, pounding away at her pillow. It was nice work.

My birthday came. Number ten. They gave me gifts my parents would have given me. They signed the card: Love, Mom and Dad and Margot. "Margot" even threw a spectacularly authentic tantrum while we were cutting the cake. She locked herself in the bathroom for three hours, flushing the toilet over and over to run up "Dad's" water bill.

The summer wore on. I tried to act normally, but I worried about my real parents and sister. If they were held captive somewhere. If they were dead.

I'd lie in bed at night, my windows open, listening to the neighbors' backyard bug light zapping mosquitoes. Thousands of mosquitoes a night. A mosquito genocide. I'd force myself to stay awake past a point when I was sure the three of them, downstairs in the living room watching TV, would assume that I was asleep, and then I would listen with straining ears to their commercial-break conversation, trying to pick out details of their plan and news of my real family. But I was always defeated by exhaustion, and fell asleep before I heard anything.

My first attack came one night in July. I woke up sweating and shaking, the bed rocking in time with my newly-thin body. My head was saying: *Oh no oh no oh no*. I thought I was having a heart attack or a stroke. I thought that I'd been successfully poisoned. I grabbed my head and held on until the sun came up. I didn't know what else to do. There was no one in that house I could call to for help.

Making it until morning was no comfort. Nothing changed. I was still a hostage. An attack woke me almost every night after. Eventually I learned how to fall asleep during them.

Autumn arrived, crisp and smoky. Jacket weather. Homework weather. School began again. Fifth grade. My "parents" became "concerned" by my behavior—my insomnia and the ceaseless questions about family history. They looked up a doctor in the yellow pages. They took me to a dull, brown professional building by the interstate. Dentists, travel agents, a jazzercise studio.

Every Tuesday evening I spent fifty minutes telling the therapist what I was so nervous about while "Mom" and "Dad" and "Margot" had dessert at the Denny's across the highway. I made fears up—girls, germs, the bullies at school. We completed exercises in a paperback workbook. *What Makes Me Feel This Way.* I never told the therapist the truth. I never told her that my family had been replaced by imposters. She would have thought I was crazy.

Back on the midway, belly full of egg salad, head on right.

This kid is lost. I know the look. The wild panic. She's searching the crowd for her parents. She's trying not to cry. She's saying *um, um, um, um*, over and over like she's just realized she made a terrible mistake but doesn't know how to fix it.

She's so tiny that even kneeling I tower over her, so I lie on the ground beside her while she turns in a slow circle, looking through the jungle of legs for familiar knees. *Um, um, um, um.* The crowd detours around us. The girl doesn't acknowledge that I'm here, except to place a small hand on the side of my fuzzy head while she searches. I lie there and she keeps her hand on my head until her mother finally comes crashing through the crowd, screaming the girl's name. The mother scoops the girl up, and now the girl starts to cry. Feels safe enough to cry. The mother smacks the girl on the top of the head. You scared me, she says. You scared me. She carries the girl away, stepping over me as she goes.

It had been six months since that morning in the garage. Since the imposters had taken over. I had started to give up hope that I'd ever see my real family again. Even worse, I'd begun to accept the imposters as a kind of surrogate.

I haunted the school library in the afternoons, trying to find answers. I told my "parents" I was staying late because I'd joined the Glee Club. I looked through psychology texts, the ones reserved for eighth and ninth graders. I found myself in these books. These books said that in hostage situations, after a time, some captives begin to form attachments to their captors. Begin to rely on their captors. Begin to fear that their captors will leave them. This condition is known, medically, as: Stockholm Syndrome.

I found myself in these books.

A Friday night at the beginning of that December. Light flurry of fat snowflakes in the air. Big blue moon sitting above the newly frosted lawns of the neighborhood. The phone rang. I lived and died by the clear, sustained ring of the white wall phone in the kitchen. The phone meant news from the outside world—might mean news of my real family.

I rushed for the receiver, but "Mom" beat me to it. She talked while I cleared the dinner table and "Dad" and "Margot" washed and dried the dishes. I watched her face for signs of news, of a change, of new orders issued. But it was just Mrs. Blume, my best friend Max's mother from across the street, offering to take Max and me to a movie.

I didn't want to go. Something didn't feel

right. That *thing* began to work its way up my spine. I couldn't breathe. I stood in the middle of the kitchen, shaking like an old man.

"Mom" knelt in front of me. "Honey, what is it?" she asked. "What's wrong?"

I had to tell them. I had to. I was exhausted. I had no idea of the effort required to live in constant fear.

"I have these thoughts," I said. "Dad" and "Margot" stopped their work at the sink and turned to listen. "I have these thoughts and I think you're not who you say you are. I think you're somebody else."

"Who do you think we are?" "Mom" asked.

I was crying. Tears and snot streamed from my eyes and nose. "I don't know," I said.

"Oh, honey, come here." "Mom" pulled me in, wrapping her arms around me. She smelled like my mother, she felt like my mother. Her tears on my cheek were so much like my mother's tears. I hugged her, holding on as tightly as I could. I shook and shook and shook. "Margot" knelt down beside us and put her arms around me as well. "Dad" came over and put his hand on my shoulder.

"It's just us," "Mom" whispered, her breath hot in my ear. "Just your family. Nobody different."

It broke like a fever. My delusion. The big, wracking sobs came again, but this time they were a relief. Mom and Margot hugged me tighter, and my dad knelt and put his arms around all of us.

"You've had such a tough time lately," my mom said. "But it's going to be okay. You'll see."

We stayed like that for a while, in that embrace on the kitchen floor. Then I went upstairs to the bathroom and wiped away my tears and snot and splashed cold water on my face. I felt so foolish. I couldn't believe that I had done this to myself, and to them. I resolved to make it up to them, to be the best son and brother I could be. I made myself a promise in the bathroom mirror.

I went down to the foyer and put on my coat and hat and gloves and blue-and-gray moon boots. They all came down to see me off. I kissed my mom and dad and sister goodbye and ran across to the Blume's driveway, slipping and sliding on the long, shiny patches of black ice in the road. I found Max and Mrs. Blume in a cloud of gray exhaust, chipping frost from the windshield of their idling minivan.

I looked back at my house. My family stood in the front picture window, arms around each other's shoulders, smiling and waving. I smiled and waved back.

TWO

Whenever Mrs. Blume called and offered to take me and Max to something that was supposed to be fun, I knew it was a bribe. I knew it meant: Grandpa Blume. I knew it meant: Ferndale.

People from my town generally tried to avoid Ferndale. None of our parents worked in the steel factory, with its flame-topped smokestacks belching soot, or in the chemical plant, with its rusty drainpipes discharging sludge into the lake. We didn't know any of the ragged, wild kids who went to Ferndale Middle School. One of our science teachers used to lived there, but a year or so before he had been dragged out of his classroom by the police for touching Mike Bogomonie's penis.

It always seemed to be night in Ferndale, or at least very dark. Strange birds filled the sky. Bats, maybe. Homeless people wandered the streets. Stray dogs, mangy and rabid-eyed, roamed in packs, barking and yowling. There was trash everywhere—styrofoam cups and sale flyers and condom wrappers blown up against the fences surrounding the vacant lots and dilapidated buildings. There was a down-on-its-luck K-Mart, a glass-and-steel Titanic in a sea of crippled, upset shopping carts. There was a 24-hour adult video and magazine shop, its windows and glass front door painted an impenetrable black. There was a roller-skating rink, which we'd been told had once been a city-wide center of teenage social interaction, but that no one I knew was allowed to visit under any circumstances. A different section of it burned to the ground every six months. My dad said it kept the local insurance companies in business.

The Blume's kept their grandfather in a dreary high-rise nursing home behind the K-Mart. Every few weeks Mrs. Blume paid him a quick visit and she had me come along to keep Max company. Afterwards, she would take us for ice cream or to look through the toy aisles of the K-Mart or to see a movie at the Tinsel Town theatre. Some kind of reward.

All his life, Grandpa Blume had been a

captain or a colonel in the army. Something important. Max told me that he had secretly been in the CIA, in charge of spying on the Russians, but Mrs. Blume told us that that wasn't true, and Grandpa Blume was just telling tales.

Max talked about his grandfather all the time. He made up stories about him saving the country from the Russians. Whenever we played soldiers, Max took Grandpa Blume's big old Army jacket and cap out of the Blume's hall closet and pretended he was a spy.

But Max always got nervous when we were in the nursing home. Antsy. Standing in the sea-green lobby under the bright fluorescent lights; checking in with the hollow-eyed, unwell-looking man behind the sliding receptionist's window; riding up in the tiny elevator; walking down the hall toward Grandpa Blume's room. Squeak, squeak, squeak. Our sneakers on the linoleum. All the way, Max would talk at a mile-a-minute about anything that came into his head—school, comic books, the movie we were going to see. Anything but his grandfather. A mile-a-minute. Hey, remember this. Hey, did you know this. Mrs. Blume always had to tell him to shush because people in the rooms we were passing were trying to sleep.

Max got nervous because: sometimes Grandpa Blume was not himself.

We got to the room. Max stopped talking. Mrs. Blume quietly turned the knob and opened the door.

It was dark inside, except for a string of multi-colored Christmas lights scotch-taped around the single window in the far wall. The lights blinked on and off. Whenever they blinked on, I could see Grandpa Blume.

He lay on his back in the bed, arms at his sides. Thin as a rail, still as a corpse. His eyes and mouth were open. The sheets and blanket were tucked around him so tightly it seemed like whoever made the bed was trying to keep him in place.

Grandpa Blume sat up, slowly. The blanket peeled away from the bed like a layer of skin.

"Who's there?" he said. He had a scared little boy's voice.

"Just me, dad," Mrs. Blume said. She walked into the room and clicked on the light by his bed. "Just your daughter."

Grandpa Blume squinted at us in the new light.

"I brought you some books." Mrs. Blume set a stack of used paperbacks on the bedside table. Grandpa Blume liked to have men's adventure novels read to him. A bookcase under the window was full of them. All of the covers featured the same grimacing, dark-haired man, but on each cover the man was holding a different type of gun.

"Who else is with you?" Grandpa Blume said. His head nodded up and down all the time, like he was constantly agreeing with somebody. "Who's that by the door?"

Mrs. Blume came back to us and gave Max a little nudge. "Go say hello to your grandfather."

Max shuffled up to the edge of the bed, eyes on the floor, hands in his pockets. "Hi, Grandpa," he said.

Grandpa Blume leaned in so that his face was almost touching Max's. He put his spotted, shaky hands over Max's ears and moved Max's head around, looking at him from different angles. Grandpa Blume looked confused. He shook his head and whispered something to himself over and over. I couldn't hear what he was saying, so I took a step in.

What he was saying was: *Who the fuck is this? Who the fuck is this?*

He finally gave up and looked to Mrs. Blume. His eyes were wet, and his lower lip was trembling.He looked like he was going to cry. So did Max.

"I don't know who this is." Grandpa Blume said.

"It's Max, Dad." Mrs. Blume looked like she was going to cry, too. "My son Max. Your grandson. You remember."

Grandpa Blume didn't look convinced. "Max," he said, slowly, stretching out the word. "*Maaaaaaax.*" Max took a step back and huddled against his mother.

Mrs. Blume put a hand on the back of my neck and moved me in next to the bed. "And you remember the Blaylocks," she said, "from across the road. This is their son, Huddie. He's come to visit before."

Grandpa Blume squinted at me. Something clicked for him. In his eyes. He nodded, once, a real nod. "Of course," he said. "I know him. I know him."

Mrs. Blume pushed me closer to the edge of the bed. I wasn't sure what to say. I knew that my parents had come to visit him the week before, for Thanksgiving. I could see the card they'd given him on the nightstand next to his cigarettes.

"My parents were here last week," I said. "They brought you a card."

Grandpa Blume reached out. I thought he was going to grab me, but instead he pulled a cigarette from the pack and brought it up to his lips. Mrs. Blume said, "Dad…" but he waved her off. He tore a match from a matchbook and ran it back and forth over the flint strip on the back until it finally caught. He touched the match to the tip of the cigarette and sucked on the end, pulling his cheeks in even deeper. He held the smoke inside of him. When he exhaled, it came out in two long, steady streams through his nostrils.

He looked back up at me. All traces of the fear were gone from his face. His eyes were clear and blue. "Who was here?" he said.

"My parents," I said. "The Blaylocks. They gave you that card."

Grandpa Blume ran his tongue across the ridge of his gums, where his teeth should have been. He found a tiny piece of tobacco stuck at the front, flicked it loose with the end of his tongue and swallowed it. "I know who your parents are," he said. His voice was getting stronger and deeper. It sounded like a man's voice. "Your father with that pipe."

I nodded. "That's right."

He shook his head. "They didn't come to visit."

"Of course they did, Dad," Mrs. Blume said. "They gave you that card."

Grandpa Blume cleared his throat, dredging something up from inside his chest. He turned his head and spat a brown wad into a plastic kidney-shaped dish on his nightstand. "That isn't who came to visit me. I don't know who those people were."

"They were the Blaylocks, Dad," Mrs. Blume said.

"I don't know who those people were," he said. His voice was firm and sure. He sat back in bed and took another drag. "What they were up to."

"Who were they?" I said.

He blew the smoke out through his nostrils. "Fuck if I know, boy."

"Dad, you're just—" Mrs. Blume put her hand on my chest and moved me back from the bed. "He doesn't remember," she said. " Sometimes he gets confused."

That *thing* on the base of my spine. Crawling up.

"I'm not confused," Grandpa Blume said. He didn't look confused.

"Well, I'm not going to argue with you, Dad."

"Goddamn right you're not going to argue with me. I know what I saw. Spent forty years looking for that kind of shit. I know when people are lying to me."

"Of course you do, Dad."

I stepped back toward the doorway.

"Max, maybe you should turn on the TV for Grandpa," Mrs. Blume said. "The remote control's over on the nightstand."

Max didn't move.

"*Wheel of Fortune*," Grandpa Blume said. "Time for the *Wheel of Fortune*."

The thing had taken over. It shook inside and I shook outside. My head said: *call home call home call home*.

I turned and ran out into the hall, down to the elevators. I stabbed at the button, but it didn't come and it didn't come so I pushed through the door into the stairwell and raced down to the first floor, nearly tripping at every landing, my footfalls echoing all around me.

Out into the sickly brightness of the lobby. There was a pay phone on the wall in one corner, its metal face scarred with angry gouges and obscene etchings. It ate three dimes before I gave up and turned to the man behind the reception window. He snorted when I asked to use his phone. He told me that management had had it fixed to receive outside calls only, to prevent the "help" from spending their shifts racking up long-distance charges. He spun a few numbers on the dial and held up the dead receiver as proof. My head said: *call home call home call home*. I opened the lobby's front door and ran outside.

A rawness out on the sidewalk—the raw, biting chill in the air; the raw brick faces of the closed shops along the street, every window dark. I looked for a gas station, an open restaurant. Nothing. Even the K-Mart was closed.

Finally, at the corner, a sign overhead. A blue bell in a circle. *Public Telephone*. Buzzing neon beside it. *Girls, Novelties, 25 cent Viewing Booths*.

I pulled open the door. Inside: bright lights and warmth. Inside: tall shelves of cardboard video boxes screaming pink, a row of men flipping pages at a stand of magazines.

There was an open doorway at the back of

the room. A dark hallway stretched beyond. Muffled music, women's screams, men's grunts from unseen rooms on either side of the hall. The pay phone was mounted on the wall at the hall's end, under the red light of an exit sign. Another sign beside the phone, a mother's admonition. Clean Up After Yourselfs.

I charged for the end of the hall. I tried to keep my eyes on the phone, on the exit sign, but many of the curtains covering the rooms were pulled back or wide open. And so I saw.

Men sat slumped in the booths, lit by flickering TV screens, slacks around their ankles, right hands working furiously, eyes shut tight, heads back, mouths open. On the screens, images of women held down, their faces lost in pillows, in men's naked laps. The women screamed and jerked, mouths full, pounded at from behind, in front, on top. The violence was astonishing. I wished myself blind, but my sight never failed.

I ran headlong into the pay phone wall and fell to my knees. I stood, digging furiously in my pocket for my last dime. I reached up and pushed the coin into the slot.

The ring tone purred in my ear. One ring. Two rings. Three. I could see the phone in our kitchen, its bell sounding clearly in the empty house. It was eight o'clock on a Friday night. My parents had never spent a weekend night away from home. I knew. I knew. My head said: *Stupid stupid stupid stupid.*

I started yelling in my little voice, No no no no no. The women in the booths yelled with me, Yes yes yes yes yes. The hall filled with the sound. I banged the receiver against the phone. The men in the booths whipped into a frenzy. Their grunts grew in time with the yelling, with the banging, climbing to a moan, peaking in screams.

You can panic in one of these costumes. Pretty easily. It can sneak up on you and take over. Just like that.

Even if you aren't claustrophobic, imagine being inside. The weight of the costume, heavy on your shoulders, on your back. The heat. The sweat on your forehead, in your armpits, in your crotch, running down your legs in slow streams. Being unable to wipe it away, or scratch the itches it creates. The muffled noise of the Park—the screaming, the yelling, the endless loops of bright carnival music. The sound of your breathing, loud and labored in the big head. The smell of your breath brought back to you, hot on your face. What it smells like: rust and gasoline. What it smells like: Fear.

It usually happens on the midway. All that open space. The *thing* crawls up my spine, cold and wet. And right when I think I can control it, that I can keep it calm, I realize that it's rabid. Frothing at the mouth. Shaking and tearing and lashing with its teeth and claws and tail. My hands go wild with it. The muscles of my face. A Parkinsonian tremor. The thing runs screaming through me, knocking the furniture around, threatening to bring me to my knees. My head says: *blahblahblahblahblah*. I have to use all of my strength to keep from flying apart, to keep from going completely insane.

There's a little boy pulling on my tail. I reach blindly for his hand with my giant paw. His mother snaps a picture. He tries to pull away but

I keep his hand in my paw. His mother snaps another picture. I keep his hand in my paw. I hold on.

And then I see him, over by the pay phones. With the military build, with the brush cut, with the mustache. With the aviator sunglasses. With the pipe.

I ran out of the porn shop, back to the nursing home, tears freezing on my cheeks. Max and Mrs. Blume stood out front under the awning, worried. I pleaded, gasping and sobbing.

"Please," I begged. "Take me home."

The ride back. The barren interstate. The quiet of my town. A long blur of streetlights, traffic lights, fast-food restaurants lit from inside, their booths empty, uniformed teenagers slouching behind the counters, waiting, watching the clocks. Mrs. Blume reprimanding me the entire way. Mrs. Blume driving so unforgivably slowly.

We pulled onto our street. Down through the birch trees. Mrs. Blume still reprimanding. I wasn't listening. I wanted to open the door and jump from the car and run the rest of the way. I wanted to open the door and jump from the car and run off into the night. I didn't want to see what I knew was coming.

The Blume's house appeared on the left, the light of the TV flickering in the living room window. My house appeared on the right.

The windows were dark. The driveway was empty. The front door stood open, letting the night into the house.

Mrs. Blume parked the minivan and sent Max home. She followed me inside the house. I turned on the foyer light. I had expected it for so long, but the reality still nearly knocked me to my knees: every coat in the closet, every shoe from the corner by the garage door—gone.

We walked slowly through the house. Neither of us said a word. The television gone, the couch gone. The kitchen table and chairs. The cupboards bare. Upstairs, my parent's room, my sister's room. Pictures taken from the walls. Beds gone, dressers gone, closets vacant. Mrs. Blume stood in the hallway between the bedrooms, silent, hand over her open mouth.

The door to my room was closed. I put my hand on the knob, turned, pushed. The bottom of the door shushed across the carpeting. I reached up on the wall and switched on the light. My bed, my dresser, my desk, my bookshelf of *Choose-Your-Own-Adventure*s and *Encyclopedia Brown*s, my stuffed animals, my wrestling pictures, my third-place plaque—all still there, untouched. Left behind.

You'd be surprised how many men with mustaches and aviator sunglasses also smoke pipes. Of that age. More than a few. But I always have to check. I always have to make sure it isn't him.

There's a commotion by the pay phones. Women screaming, men cheering, a couple of yelled cuss words. I push my way through the crowd, dragging the boy behind me. His mother says something that I don't hear. A writhing human wave crashes over us. I hold tight onto the boy's hand but lose sight of the man with the pipe.

A moose is attacking a pirate.

The moose is pummeling the pirate with his hooves—clapping him on the sides of the head, smacking him in the face. The pirate falls to the ground. His plastic parrot skitters across the pavement. He raises his peg leg, trying to kick the moose in its exposed gut, but the moose tucks its head and starts ramming the prone pirate with its wooden antlers.

Adults are yelling for help. Kids are crying. Teenagers are clapping and whooping, crowding in around the fight. I can't see the man with the pipe.

"Fuckin' Cuban bastard!" the pirate yells. *Fookin' Cuban bastard.* And then the moose gores the pirate in the mouth with its antlers.

Someone grabs me by the shoulders and spins me around. A woman, lip-sticked face pressed into mine. "Do something!" she screams. I push her out of the way and pull the boy in close behind me, shoving through the innermost ring of cheering teenagers.

Ilford's splayed on the ground, bleeding from his nose and mouth. A few of his teeth sit on the pavement beside him. He's waving the parrot like some kind of weapon. He's screaming at the moose. "Come on, you greasy Cuban bastard!"

It looks like the moose caught something in the eye. The peg leg. The socket is dark with blood. The fur is matted. He's got one hoof up, covering. He's swinging wildly with the other hoof, stumbling in disoriented circles. "Kill you," he's saying. "Kill you for this."

It's the man with the pipe. He steps between them. He spreads his arms out like wings, palms up. "Enough," he says. "Enough."

I spent that night at the Blume's, awake in Max's bed while he slept in a camping bag on the floor. I heard Mrs. Blume quizzing Mr. Blume downstairs. He'd fallen asleep in his recliner with the Pacers' game and the last can of a Pabst six-pack. He hadn't seen a thing. She made phone calls from the kitchen. She called every one of our neighbors, apologizing for the late hour. No one had seen or heard anything. Curtains had been drawn, televisions had been turned up. *The Love Boat. Fantasy Island.*

It didn't seem possible that three people could pack up and move all of their possessions in the span of two hours. But there it was across the road: my empty house. I could see it from Max's window. The front door still gaping. Mrs. Blume had closed it as we left, but I'd turned back and opened it again.

The police came. By morning's light we found signs that the operation hadn't proceeded as smoothly as we'd thought the night before. Deep tire tracks rutted the lawn where a large truck had backed up to the front door. Muddy shoeprints trailed up the stairs. The remnants of a few broken plates lay in the sink.

That night, in a corner of the cellar where the washer and dryer once sat, where my dad's workbench stood without its tools, I found a red Thom McCann shoebox. Inside the box was a cassette that, when played later, featured all four of our voices, telling jokes and singing songs on the trip to Florida. Inside the box was a golf pencil and a little spiral notebook, the names and distances of each street we traveled down printed out in neat capital letters. Inside the box was a photograph, taken by a salesman at one of the motel pools. Margot and I dripping in our swimsuits, my mom with her Jackie Collins paperback, my dad with his sunglasses, with his notebook, with his pipe.

My house went up for auction a few months later. The Pratt's moved in with their basketball hoop and their two brutal, bullying sons. The Blume's adopted me, and converted their cellar into a bedroom. I kept all of my old things— my desk, my bookshelves, my third-place plaque. I slept in my tiny bed long after my feet hung over the end. Once a month, we'd visit Grandpa Blume in the nursing home. He always asked me if I'd found my parents yet.

Every morning, long before the neighborhood awoke, I got up and walked to the end of my new family's driveway. I looked down the road in each direction. I waited for a few minutes, and when nothing came I would go back inside and get ready for another day.

Men always respond to a dad's voice. No matter how old the men are. No matter whose dad it is. They stop fucking around.

The moose's head is bowed. He's covering his bloody eye socket with a hoof. He's crying. He's saying, "I can't see. I can't see."

The man with the pipe puts a hand on the moose's shoulder. "You need to go get some help," he says. His rumbling baritone. The moose nods and turns and walks back toward the first-aid station. The crowd gives him a wide berth.

Fookin' Cuban bastard.

The man with the pipe turns to Ilford. "You need to watch your mouth," he says. Ilford watches his mouth. Ilford picks up his teeth and his parrot and gets to his feet and hobbles away on his peg leg.

Park Security arrives, but the only people to yell at are the teenagers. "Move along," they say to the teenagers. "Move along." The teenagers disperse.

The man with the pipe dropped his sunglasses at some point. He bends to pick them up, slowly, at the knees, favoring his lower back. I'm shaking again—my hands and legs and the muscles in my face. *Blahblahblahblahblah,* says my head, so I pull it off. It comes away easily this time.

The man with the pipe is crouched on the ground. He looks up at me.

"Oh," he says.

I ran away when I was sixteen. I hitched rides and hopped Greyhounds, moving south. I followed the route in the notebook. I stopped at those three motels. I checked into the same rooms. I quizzed the staff. I showed the picture. I sat out by the empty pools. I waited for as long as my money held, but nothing came.

After a few weeks, I made it here. I got a room at the Gilbert Transient Hotel just off the highway. Bed, desk, chair, black and white television. A strong shower curtain rod where I can do my pull-ups. A tall doorframe where I can hang the heavy bag. It has been fine. It has been all that I need.

I took whatever jobs were available at the Park. I cleaned restrooms, sold concessions, tore tickets. I worked my way up through the ranks. I kept my eyes open. I sent a postcard to the Blumes, thanking them for their kindness. The postcard was: Diggity Dawg surrounded by wolves and dragons and pirates and ghosts, standing in front of the Park's carousel.

I had to come back. Remember: the last thing that I said to my dad was, *I hate you*.

We made a deal, my family and I, when we were here on our trip. I play the cassette every night in my room before the shaking comes and maybe I sleep and maybe I don't. On the cassette I hear us making the deal. Voices from eight years ago. My parents insisting and my sister and I agreeing. We were pulling into the Park's massive lot. We were buzzing with excitement.

"If we get separated, we'll meet by the carousel," my dad says through the hiss on the tape. "And no matter how long it takes, stay there and wait. I'll find you."

We all agree. We make a promise.

Behind the man with the pipe is the bank of pay phones and behind the bank of pay phones is the carousel.

"You made it," I say.

The man with the pipe stands. "I did," he says. "I made it."

He looks like I thought he would. There's a little extra weight pushing at the belly of his shirt, but besides that he looks fit and healthy. I can see the muscles of his forearms work when he handles his pipe. He's got a full head of slate-gray hair. His mustache is gray, too.

"You look like I thought you would," he says. Of course I do. With a lot of work, I've become the young man in the picture that used to be on our mantle. I'm even missing a tooth, like him, courtesy of the Pratt's older son.

"Where's Mom? Where's Margot?" I say. I'm babbling, the words coming too fast, pouring out of my mouth, bouncing on the pavement. I want to grab his shoulders. I want to put my arms around his shoulders and squeeze. We're the same height.

The man with the pipe looks down at the boy beside me. "Who's this?" he says.

"I don't know," I say. I let go of his hand but the boy stays beside me.

"I'm Carl," the boy says.

The man with the pipe smiles. "Hello, Carl."

"You made it," I say, calmer, catching my breath.

"Of course I did. I finally remembered." The man with the pipe looks over his shoulder. "Meet in front of the carousel."

I can't help but smile. He sounds just like he did on the tape. I haven't cried since that night in the kitchen, but I feel like I'm going to cry now. Feel safe enough to cry.

"I waited for a long time," I say.

He looks back at me. He's still smiling and I smile wider, even though I feel like crying. His smile is contagious.

"Hey," he says. "Would your old man let

you down?"

It's amazing how quickly you can move in these costumes. My paw fits perfectly around his throat. He spits and gurgles. His face fills with blood.

"Where are they?" I'm screaming, my face an inch from his. "*Wherearetheywherearetheywherearethey???*"

The man with the pipe is turning blue. He's trying to say something, but my giant thumb is pressing into his windpipe. Mandible shift, masseter contraction, tensing of the superior pterygoid. He's swallowing his tongue. Very important, watching them swallow.

The woman who grabbed me earlier is running through the midway, waving her arms. "Jesus Christ," she screams, "the animals are attacking! The animals have gone wild!"

"*Where are they???*"

"Blaylock, for the love of God!" Jensen grabs my arm from behind. A couple of park security goons pull me off the man with the pipe. One of the goons is the same size I am in my costume.

He pins me to the ground and sits on my chest. It's hard to breathe. The man with the pipe sinks to his knees and coughs and hacks, clutching his throat.

Jensen shoves Carl away with the other goon. "Get this boy back to his mother," he says.

"Don't!" I scream after them. "Don't! None of these parents are real!"

But the goon lands a blow to my head and my head hits the concrete and—

THREE

He asked if I was hungry and I said I guessed so and he asked if I knew any-place to get a decent breakfast this late and I said I guessed so. There's a diner not far from the Park, wedged underneath the upward slope of the interstate on-ramp. He drove us in the Pontiac station wagon. It was the first time I'd ever sat in the front seat.

He asked me if I wanted to go home and change and I said no, that this was fine if he didn't mind the smoke smell. He said he didn't. Jensen told me just to keep the costume, on account of the smoke smell and the fact that he wanted me out of the Park immediately if this man wasn't go-ing to press charges, but that I could be sure the cost of the costume would come out of my final paycheck, which they'd send in the mail so don't set foot in this place again, Blaylock you psycho-path.

Fookin' nutjob. Ilford escorted us to the gates of the park. "So long, Blaylock, you tosser." He had a lisp when his tongue poked through the new gap in his front teeth. *Tho long, Blaylock.*

Evening has come. The sky's gone soft and pink. The man with the pipe and I sit on opposite sides of a booth by a window. He sets his pipe in an ashtray next to the napkin dispenser. I get a few looks because of the costume, but living in this town people get used to seeing these kinds of things.

The waitress brings us coffee and eggs and bacon and the man with the pipe says, "Bring my boy a steak for his eye. Raw." I don't know which eye he's talking about because both eyes are black from when my head hit the ground but all the hairs on the back of my neck stand up when he says *My boy.*

"I'm not your boy."

"Not technically, no." He digs into his eggs, cutting and spearing and feeding himself in the same motion. My dad never ate that way. The man with the pipe has given up all pretense of playing the part.

"I thought you were hungry," he says

through a mouthful of food.

"I changed my mind." The waitress brings me a plate with a cold t-bone in a little pool of blood. I tell her she can keep the plate and I take the steak and press it into my right eye. It feels good and cool and the skin on my eyelid and around my eye tingles from absorbing the iron or zinc or whatever's in the steak.

"Where are they?" I say. "My dad and my mom and Margot. What happened to them?"

He shrugs. "I don't know," he says, cutting, spearing, chewing. "We never had contact with them. They were gone when we came in."

Bump-bump. Bump-bump. Every time the cars climb onto the interstate overhead they hit a couple of seams in the pavement, *bump-bump*, *bump-bump*, and all the silverware and ketchup bottles and coffee cups on the tables rattle.

The man with the pipe steadies his cup with his hand. "My name's Gary," he says.

"You were nothing like him," I say. "I always knew."

"No you didn't. Not for a long time. You were too young."

"I remember everything," I say, pointing the steak at him. Little drops of blood spatter onto the tabletop. "I remember him right up until that night with the wrestling."

"Don't raise your voice," he says. "What night with the wrestling?"

"The night you replaced them. There were wrestling matches and we didn't go. I told him I hated him."

The man with the pipe stops chewing. He looks at me, holding his food in his mouth.

"That wasn't it," he says.

"What wasn't it?"

"When we replaced them. It happened long before that."

That *thing* on my spine.

"Your family vacation," he says. "A motel. Cheap place. Your dad was a real tightwad."

Crawling up.

"You're lying," I say.

The man with the pipe swallows and wipes his mouth with a napkin. "You were asleep," he says. "You were alone in the room. They'd already been removed. The women got into their bed, I got into bed next to you. You'd been swimming. Your hair was still wet."

"More coffee?" The waitress is at our table, holding up the pot.

The man with the pipe pushes his mug to the edge of the table. "Please," he says. "Thank you."

She fills his mug, slopping a little coffee over the sides. "And for the dog?" she asks. I shake my head and she leaves.

"It was you? All that time?"

The man with the pipe nods. "I remember the night with the wrestling. Your computer. *I hate you, I hate you.*" He gives a little laugh. "I figured you'd know enough to come back here eventually. I remembered we had some kind of meeting place worked out." He pokes my steak with his fork. "Put that back up there."

I press the t-bone into my other eye.

"I've been to the park a couple of times," he says. "But I kept looking for a giant clock." He takes another bite of his eggs. "Turns out there is no giant clock at that park."

"Where are the other two?"

"I have no idea. We were debriefed and let go. We never kept in touch. That woman was a frigid bitch and that girl was a royal pain in the ass. Pardon my French." He cracks a cough into his fist. "And if you're not going to call me Dad, at least call me Gary."

"You're lucky I don't kill you."

"Don't talk that way when I'm paying for your meal." He takes a sip of his coffee. He pushes the ashtray to my side of the table. "You can smoke if you want."

"I can't reach my cigarettes."

"Where are they?"

"In my underwear."

"Use the pipe."

I put the steak down and pick up the pipe.

I tap it on the side of the ashtray, clearing the bowl. He reaches into the pocket of his shirt and takes out a pouch of tobacco and a book of matches and his little metal reamer. He places them on the table and slides them over to my side. I scrape the carbon from the sides of the bowl with the tiny shovel. I take a pinch of tobacco from the pouch and fill the pipe. I pack the tobacco into the bowl with the tamper. I've seen him do this a thousand times. He watches me closely. He nods when I'm done.

"Getting pulled off the job was as much of a surprise to me as it was to you," he says.

I put the pipe in my mouth. The stem is still wet from his saliva. My teeth fit perfectly into the marks on the mouthpiece.

"And for the record," he says. "I knew you never hated me."

He lights a match and reaches across the table. I lean in. The little flame touches the to-bacco in the bowl. I suck on the pipe until the tobacco catches and my mouth fills with smoke. I inhale, holding the smoke in my lungs. My head goes light. That thing on my spine calms down and settles in.

He shakes out the match and tosses it into the ashtray. He sits back in the booth. I blow the smoke out through my nostrils. Like a dragon.

Gary smiles.

"Perfect," he says. "My boy."

ABOUT THE AUTHOR

Scott O'Connor has worked as an actor, meat cutter, garbage man, newspaper reporter, comic book store clerk, public relations flack, tour guide, video editor and graphic designer.

He was raised in Upstate New York and lives in Los Angeles. This is his first book.